Who Will Sing A Lullaby?

by **Dee Lillegard**   illustrated by **Dan Yaccarino**

ALFRED A. KNOPF NEW YORK

"Listen to that baby cry!"
the birds around the cradle sigh.
Who will sing a lullaby?
Nightingale fluffs up her wings.
"Hush-a-bye . . . ," she softly sings.

But Crow swoops down and cocks his head.
Crow lifts Baby from the bed. . . .
"I'll take Baby flying.
That will stop the crying."

Baby in the cornfields.
Baby in the rye.
Baby's eyes begin to close
as the sun sinks down the sky.

Crow lays Baby down, asleep.
"Caw-caw!" he squawks by the cradle's side.
The birds all whisper, *"Not so loud."*
Baby's eyes open wide. . . .

"Listen to that baby cry!"
the birds around the cradle sigh.
Who will sing a lullaby?

But Goose swoops down and nods her head.
Goose lifts Baby from the bed. . . .
"*I'll* take Baby flying.
That will stop the crying."

Baby on the blue lake,
where geese and ganders fly.
Baby's eyes begin to close
as the sun sinks down the sky.

Goose lays Baby down, asleep.
"Honk-honk!" she calls by the cradle's side.
The birds all whisper, *"Not so loud."*
Baby's eyes open wide. . . .

"Listen to that baby cry!"
the birds around the cradle sigh.
Nightingale fluffs up her wings.
"Hush-a-bye. . . ," she softly sings.

But Owl swoops down and bows his head.
Owl lifts Baby from the bed. . . .
"*I'll* take Baby flying.
That will stop the crying."

Baby in the treetops.
Baby in a nest up high.
Baby's eyes begin to close
as the sun sinks down the sky.

Owl lays Baby down, asleep.
"Hoo-hoo!" he hoots by the cradle's side.
The birds all whisper, *"Not again!"*
Baby's eyes open wide. . . .

"Listen to that baby cry!"
the birds around the cradle sigh. . . .

Swan comes sweeping from her nest.
Swan holds Baby to her breast.
All the birds say, *"Swan knows best!"*

But Swan lays Baby down again.
Then . . .

"Listen to that baby cry!"
the birds around the cradle sigh.
"Won't someone sing a lullaby?"

Nightingale chirps, "May I? May I?"
Crow and Goose and Owl and Swan
say, "Nightingale, go on, go on."

Nightingale fluffs up her wings
and sings . . .

"Hush-a-bye, my Baby.
Hush. Don't cry.
Moon and stars
are shining in the sky.
Close your eyes
and have no fear.
Wings of love
are always near.
Go to sleep, my Baby,
Baby dear."

As Nightingale sings,
gentle wings
rock the cradle in soft moonbeams.
Baby Baby
dreams sweet dreams.

The birds around the cradle coo.
"Oh, Baby Baby,
we love you.
We do
we do
we do."

And soon the birds
are sleeping too. . . .

For the Nesti girls, Abigayel and Aubrey.
—D.L.

THIS IS A BORZOI BOOK PUBLISHED BY ALFRED A. KNOPF

Text copyright © 2007 by Dee Lillegard
Illustrations copyright © 2007 by Dan Yaccarino

www.randomhouse.com/kids

Educators and librarians, for a variety of teaching tools,
visit us at www.randomhouse.com/teachers

Library of Congress Cataloging-in-Publication Data
Lillegard, Dee.
Who will sing a lullaby? / by Dee Lillegard ; illustrated by Dan Yaccarino. —1st ed.
    p. cm.
SUMMARY: A group of well-meaning birds attempts to lull a crying baby to sleep.
ISBN 978-0-375-81573-7 (trade) — ISBN 978-0-375-91573-4 (lib. bdg.)
[1. Birds—Fiction. 2. Babies—Fiction. 3. Lullabies—Fiction. 4. Stories in rhyme.] I. Yaccarino, Dan, ill. II. Title.
PZ8.3.L6144Who 2007
[E]—dc22
2007004409

The illustrations in this book were created using gouache and airbrush on watercolor paper.
MANUFACTURED IN MALAYSIA
September 2007
10 9 8 7 6 5 4 3 2 1
First Edition